CEASED REMEMBRANCE

A JOURNEY THROUGH FLASHES

BUSHRA JAMAL

ISBN 979-888521356-1

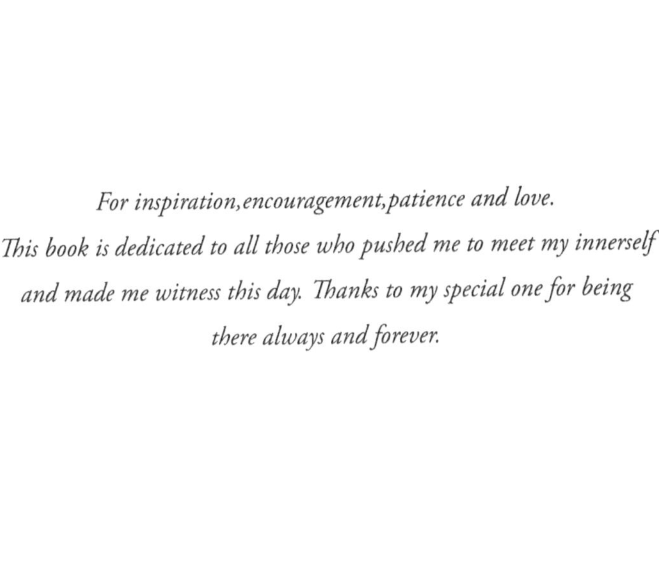

For inspiration,encouragement,patience and love.
This book is dedicated to all those who pushed me to meet my innerself
and made me witness this day. Thanks to my special one for being
there always and forever.

Contents

Preface   *vii*

  1. Content   1

"SMITHEREENS OF FORGETFULNESS"

GONE LOVE

"YEARNING THROUGH FLASHES"

Reluctancy

Grasping Rays Of Hope

My 11:11 Wish

Choked Sleep

"AN ERA OF LOVELORN"

Feets Above Clouds

Seraphic Love

Unsought Love

"A FADED MEMORY"

Preoccupied

Dawn Of December

Wandering For Solace

"RAVING MEMOIR"

REMINISCENCE

Sheets Of Demure

BLISS IN SECLUSION

CERTAINTY OF HOPE

A Silver Lining

A LOST CAUSE

Contents

"AN AUTUMN I LONGED FOR"

Preface

A memoir of an unrequited love

An erotica of longing for lover's arm

A journey of parallel souls walking along

To infinity and beyond

Met by fate but destined to separate.

This book is a collection of poems and metrical compositions for the present and upcoming generation breaking all the social norms and boundaries for those two souls who choose their friendship to be beyond love.

Is it necessary for every story to have a happy ending?

I would say, "yes" why not?

"A tale which cannot culminate to its natural set,

It is better to terminate it, without any regret".

1. CONTENT

PART I
SMITHEREENS OF FORGETFULNESS

- *Gone Love*
- *Yearning through flashes*
- *An era of Lovelorn*
- *A faded memory*

PART II
RAVING MEMOIR

- *Reminiscence*
- *Bliss in seclusion*
- *Certainty of hope*
- *A lost Cause*

PART III

- ***An Autumn I longed for***

"SMITHEREENS OF FORGETFULNESS"

GONE LOVE

It all started a couple of months back,

I confessed my heart out.

while you stamped my confession,

with a promise

that it will last till eternity;

My level of happiness rose to ecstatic,

I was stupified

unaware of the fact that love is an ephemeral journey;

Alas! you left, left me in pieces.

All that love we shared is now all that i got,

And if I try to forget ,love will remember us

Till death do us apart;

I will be yours!

-Ceased Remembrance

BIO.

"YEARNING THROUGH FLASHES"

"*While seeking answers of those unanswered goodbyes,*

I walked a thousand miles.

Following your traces you left behind,

They in a meantime got washed away;

with the waves of time.

It was then when I realised,

I already lost the path to reach you;

The day Our paths got set aside.

-Ceased remembrance"

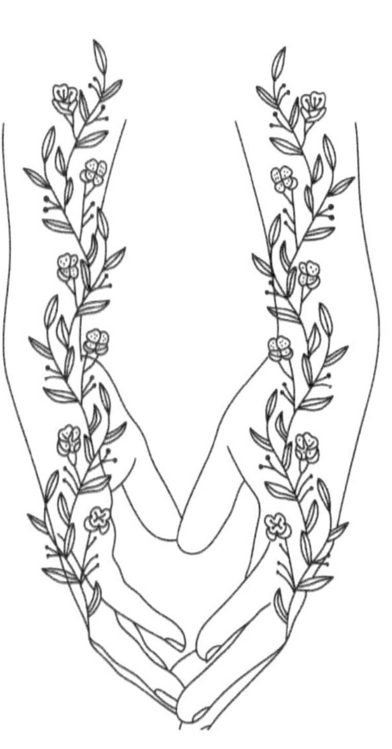

Reluctancy

"Passing by those streets where we first met

makes me reminisce things I shouldn't."

-Ceased Remembrance

"I wear your memories like i wear my flaws,

for just like them,

they are mine.

only mine.

-Ceased Remembrance"

Grasping rays of hope

"Flashes of our last memory

Reminds me of that last goodbye hug,

Sun gives to the sky while setting down

with a promise to rise again;

and in its despair, sky turns itself dark

With a Hope to see a new ray of light

After this lonely and eerie night."

-Ceased Remembrance

My 11:11 Wish

"I stayed up all night,

watching the dark sky

just to catch a shooting star

to make a wish,

to be your wish once again

even if it is for a while."

-Ceased Remembrance

Choked sleep

"The high and low notes of your zephyr breathe

I couldn't resist,

the only cure for my sleep

became the scariest hallucinations that never got healed."

-Ceased Remembrance

"*The moon can see the love*

I once buried for you,

In the depthness of the darkest night;

It gets awaken on each moonless night."

-Ceased Remembrance

"AN ERA OF LOVELORN"

Feets above clouds

"Take my soul away

Bind it with yours,

Fly with me above the clouds;

let's sit there and take some rest,

let's dance together.,

Jumping from one cloud to another.

And began our journey once again;

When the sky is clear and limitless."

-Ceased Remembrance

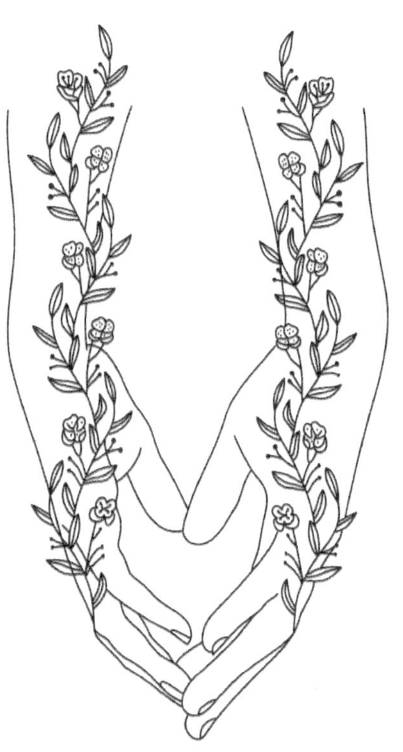

Seraphic love

For me love is poetry and poetry is him,

For me love is looking into eachother's eyes

so together we can feel the beauty of ocean and skies.

For me love is inhaling the same air he exhales

so I can read whatever he tries to hide but fails,

for me love is listening to the rythm of raindrops

so i could sing his name splashing my feet on every beat.

For me love is growing wild

so i could bloom into his garden of mind,

for me love is my heart doing a somersault while skipping a beat

every time he sends a voice note in his zephyr breathe.

For me love is writing him poetries

so he knows he lives in my thought,

For me love is leaving this incomplete.

Unsought love

There's still a hell lot of me left untouched before you leave,

Your kiss to linger on my lips,

Your fingers to caress my wounds,

Your arms to arm my soul,

Your sweet whispers saying my name,

Your presence to ease my pain.

Your warmth to elope my shivers,

Your desires to extinguish my fires,

Your willingness to dominate my mind,

Your roughness making us bind,

Your night stays and you waking up next to Mine.

Those melted candles,

and dried petals,

All over my bedsheet,

and an unpleasant fragrance,

Of the love we made,

and the left over

of our first anniversary cake.

A promising night,

witnessed by thousands of stars,

Million miles apart.

A love that remains a mystery

between You and Me,

A love that stands naked

when I am near You and You near Me,

A love to cherish,

A love to reminisce,

A love wandering in Solace,

A love disguised in faces,

A love wanting to be found,

A love roaming around.

A love hoping to meet you again,

A love echoing your name,

Please dont keep me await,

Please be back for love's sake.

Here i stand for you placidly ,

Amidst the love and hate.

Today, Tomorrow or forever,

I will Wait for you till it's whenever

-Ceased Remembrance

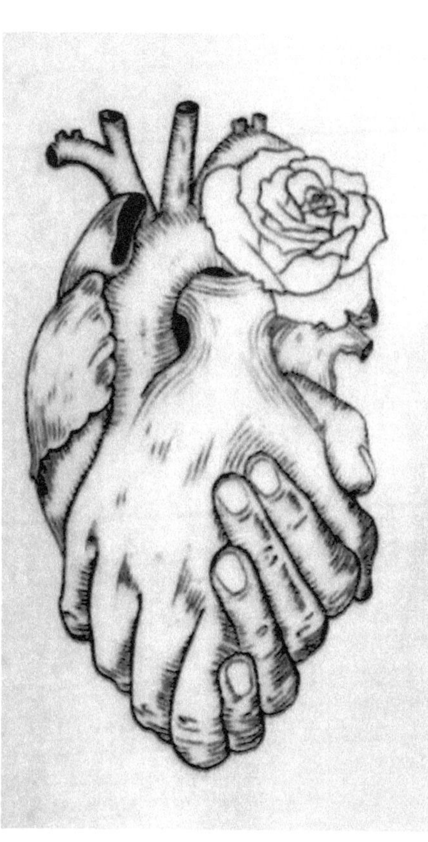

"A FADED MEMORY"

Preoccupied

"Lying on the couch,

lost in your thoughts,

your Absence makes me

Reminisce your Presence."

-Ceased Remembrance

"It's been long now since you left,

somehow i have managed ,

to come over my restlessness,

But today was the day

I collided with your thoughts,

In my absentmindedness."

-Ceased Remembrance

Dawn of December

"The broken pieces of Us,

Scratched my Soul,

I made Myself Suffer to my heart's core.

Year passed,

Season changed,

Spring Bloomed,

I placidly remained stranded,

In that December's frosty Gloom."

-Ceased Remembrance

Wandering for solace

I know You!

I once walked upon a dream with You.

We happily fell for each other.

My heart still carries your blue prints,

I still search for you,

In between those lyrics of our playlist.

Your name is hidden behind the curtains of my mind.

I remember Everything.

From your promises,

To Your bygones.

It's blurry,

It's getting vague,

Bit by Bit,

Day by Day.

Do i really know You?

Are you still there?

If yes, then where?

Was that all just a dream?

or It was something real?

Maybe,It was a dream!

A non-existing dream!

Or a surreal thought, maybe!

My soul still Shivers,

My body gets numb .

Why the hell it scares me?

Losing a fictional character,

In My own fantasy.

I wish My questions carry answers too,

If only i was still walking upon that dream with you

"RAVING MEMOIR"

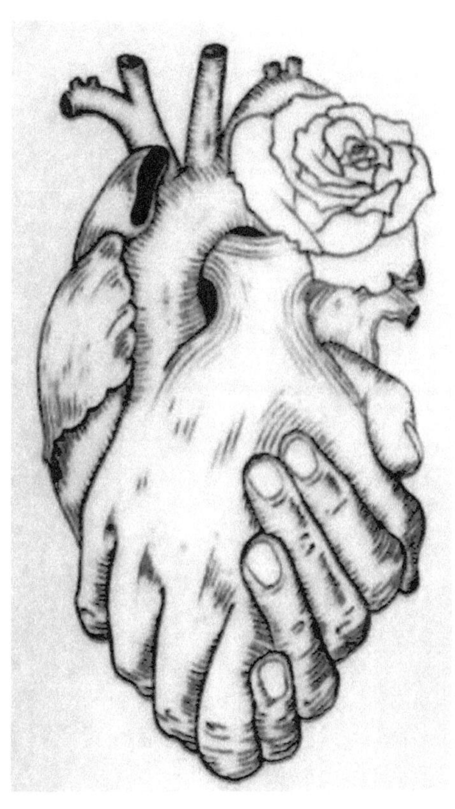

REMINISCENCE

To the person whose presence is gonna be Saudaded by Me Forever-

My Granny used to say,"you don't need to find a soul for yourself, our soul do that for us because God created us In pairs." I laughed while she smiled.

It was then when i first saw you,

my heart skipped a beat,

i realised it was all she meant,

it was all i need.

Looking at you looking at me, made me hypnotised by my destiny.

Somehow we got attached ,

And there came a time when,

all you had was nothing and all you need was me.

The feeling of being yours and you being mine,

took me on cloud nine.

I was singing and dancing like a teenage girl in her youth,

and all of a sudden my world felt apart,

like a carved snowflake loses what it possess

after falling down from the highest cloud.

You were Gone!

It wasn't about you left but the way you left,

made me wrecked.

i tried,

i tried so hard to get rid of Your thoughts

that haunt me during my sleepless nights,

my choking breathe counted on You,

I used to Weep like a starving child,

amidst those eerie caliginous nights!

With the lapse of time i got healed.

No one Knows What destiny might hold for us,

In between those attachments and this detachment

i lost a part of me

belonged to my Granny.

She told me that ,"love in it's purest form , never loses its essence

just like way the dried flowers might lose their fragrance

but is always kept in remembrance .

I tied a knot to whatever i sought,

and made a promise to myself ,

I'll keep us in my reminiscence forever.

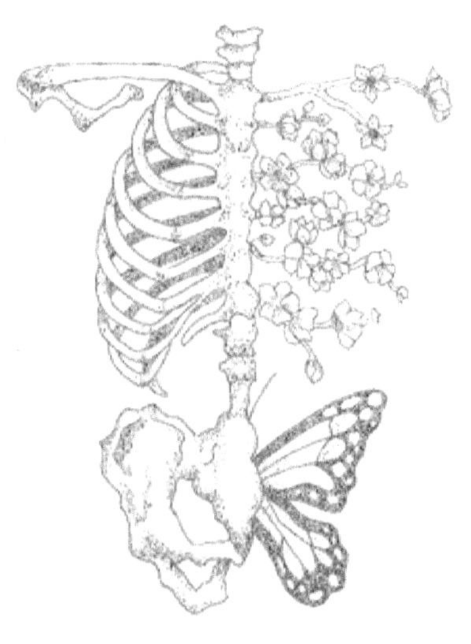

Sheets of demure

Beneath the sheets,

wrapped in the skin of vulnerability,

His zephyr breathe whispering in my ears

like a thrush singing.

My chest pressed against his,

done with the night,

Our lips still couldn't resist,

to taste each others eupehism.

The morning rays passing through the curtains,

telling us to wakeup from the night that still lingers in our mind,

reminding us we haven't finished yet

one more time,

if it pleases,

it hasn't ended yet!

BLISS IN SECLUSION

"See me closely and you will find ,

fragments of constelllations lying within my eyes."

-Ceased Remembrance

CERTAINTY OF HOPE

This isn't a story of a particuar person or a fictional character,

It's an unreal story of a rare soul made up of stars but carries just scars,

maybe from her past wounds or of the present.

Her scars were here identity for those who knew her.

She was someone strangely familiar to me.

it's been years now since i last met her before she disappeared,

from everyone's heart, from mine.

I can still feel her essence remained within me forever,

like a scented candle that gets rekindled

everytime when she tries to be herself.

All her life she strived to be herself,

her aura was made up of stars and galaxies

She wanted to live a life by her own under the shed of the limitless sky she was someone who plucked the stars of her own sky making sure that it doesn't

lose it's shine while being planted in someone else's sky.

each time she plucked a star , she gave a scar to her soul;

and then there came a moonless night,

the darkest of all she ever survived,

she died on that caliginious night,

for there was no star left on her sky

to give her a hope of light.

THOSE STARS WERE HER SHATTERED DREAMS,

THEY STILL SHINE BUT IN SOMEONE ELSE'S SKY..!!!

A silver lining

"Life seems scary

Like the darkest hour of the deepest night

You strive hard to survive,

Your anxious soul and your courageous mind,

No matter what you choose over,

To see the break of dawn you have to Fight."

-Ceased Remembrance

A LOST CAUSE

This never happened to me before,

All I have ever had and all I have ever been,

The solitary divergence in between, is nothing but a straight line i drew;

I kept cutting people of,

I was more likely to get involve into.

I ran and Ran,

looking here and there,

Figuring out things on my own,

i was all alone.

Reckless of the world I entered,

it's far more better to die;

than to get pinch by the death itself.

My hand Shivers,

My pen slips,

My words scatters,

My Heart clutches,

My Eyes bleeds

I try spinning them;

back and forth,

I am lost again,

I couldn't write anymore!

"AN AUTUMN I LONGED FOR"

This autumn that has now finally arrived;

is the one i longed for my entire life.

My life revolves around my own extraordinary Past,

carrying some hypothetical flashes of a place

I wasn't allowed to visit but I did.

It is bit difficult to be comprehended

so let's just say it has now ended.

All the leaves carrying those memories,

all the petals I watered;

refraining them to dry up,

keeping them bloom,

they withered,

making my heart gloom.

I buried my reminiscence,

inside the the safest closet of my heart,

Thowing away the key ,

I am now free,

My heart is now ready to bloom once again,

I waited for this evening,

just like a cherry blossom tree waits for spring.